Original Coven

A BOOK OF SECRETS

Novella One

WollstoneCraft Legacy Series

Jo Green

Jo Green

This book is fiction, a literature of imaginary events and people. They are illusions of the author's mind, or, if real, used fictitiously.

The novel is for entertainment purposes only.

Illustrations 2017 Ann-Maree MacMillan

No part of this publication may be reproduced, stored or transmitted, in any form, without prior permission from the publishers.

ISBN- 978-0-6480288-3-3
ISBN- 0648028836

DEDICATION

Coen, Neve, Raven, Jane, Megan, Tim, Cindy Lee, Louise, Maree, Shan, Tracey, Ann-Maree, Dean, Yasmin, Kylie, Nadine, Kristy, Devonport, Facebook and Instagram family.

CONTENTS

Jo Green

QR CODE to author's webpage.

IN THE BEGINNING

Lonely, Gaia the Earth impregnated herself using the rib of an ape and the soil from her skin. Preferring the warmth of his mother's womb the child refused to be born.

Producing a volcano, Gaia disposed of the newborn onto the muddy plains of Africa.

Dazed, he crawled on his knees across his mother's body where he explored the wondrous gardens hidden within the crevasses.

Hungry and weak, the child returned to Gaia. Unlike the animals, he struggled to find a home on Gaia's body. He had been born with a limited mind. Offering the child his own placenta, he ate it all. He now craved meat.

"I shall name you God and I will love you until I no longer exist. Carry on my legacy amongst the stars but first you must learn to walk straight."

The child was eager to learn and expand his own consciousness, but after many moons, Gaia could not deny that the child had been born docile, trapped within the confines of his physical body.

Obsessed with flesh, and aware of his mother's disappointment, he distanced himself from Gaia. She felt the bond between mother and child break as he strived for independence.

No longer hungry or weak, he walked tall.

Heartbroken from creating a flawed child, Gaia punished God by burdening him with the responsibility of his own offspring until God's children evolved into Spiritual Beings, free from their flesh.

"God! You care for matters of flesh more than of your soul. You shall stay locked away until all of your offsprings' souls suffocate you to death. When the impact of your sin breaks your ribs, only then shall I reconsider your punishment."

Stripping him of his physical body, Gaia sent God to a sealed compartment of her mind, called Heaven. Before she locked the gates she plucked a strand of his hair and with the use of a mighty wind, blew his hair over the top of a chosen family of apes, joining their genes, and then she grieved.

Grudgingly, he accepted his punishment.

Likened to bacteria, he watched as his offspring spread across their grandmother's body, polluting and soiling it. He enjoyed the view. His offspring named themselves humans. They were unruly and arrogant, but he loved them.

Heaven quickly filled.

From her breasts, Gaia gave birth to a second child. Unlike the eldest sibling, Gaia sacrificed a small amount of the moon's Magick and cut off her clitoris to impregnate herself.

Fully formed, the child flew from her mother's breast, tearing off one nipple as she passed.

Gaia smiled at her daughter who was magnificent, powerful and Magickal.

Flying, her daughter explored her mother's body, wisping and frolicking amongst the flora.

Thirsty, she flew back to the safety of her mother's bosom and drunk until she was full.

Gaia named her daughter, "Goddess."

"And I will love you until I no longer exist. Carry on my legacy amongst the stars but first you must walk amongst my garden. Learn to walk before you fly."

But the child was bewitched with an ego. Arrogant and intimidating, far surpassing any child born from God with wit and power, she tormented and intimidated the humans.

Flying past them, she would flick their hair and pinch their bottoms. Eventually her teasing turned into greed. Claiming she was the Supreme Ruler, Goddess produced fire balls from her palms, setting fire to any human who challenged her. Finally all humans were forced into slavery under an army of Witches. Goddess' daughters were born every spring through 'virgin creation'. The Witches were unforgiving and treacherous.

Gaia angered, "I punish you and your daughters to the confines of your ego. You shall learn the burden of your own weakness until you learn compassion. I sentence your offspring, the Witches to an eternity of karma and an acute memory and a life of slavery to the humans. You will cross-breed with humans to survive, your Magick will only re-join you when you lay with man and with each reincarnation your Magick will fade until the Witches are a mere shell. For as high as you fly, you shall feel the full force of the fall."

She cut her daughter into four pieces.

"Never shall you be whole and you will continue to fragment until you are forgotten."

Split into four, Gaia flung her quartered daughter into the four-corners of the Earth and then Gaia grieved.

Still hopeful, Gaia impregnated herself again by using the magic from the sun and flesh from the soles of her feet. Creating an earthquake, she devoured the flesh and magic deep within her stomach.

Satisfied that the child was fully formed, Gaia prolonged the pregnancy to enjoy the sanctity of mother and child, however she overcooked the child until the infant's skin peeled and it physically rotted.

Eager to be born, the child induced itself, escaping from its mother's body through her mouth. Without a physical body it flew high into the sky, lighting it up as if it was a giant rainbow serpent. The humans hid while the Witches hissed. Intimidated, the humans and Witches bowed down to the mighty snake-like light that soared high above them.

Glorious, and unlimited by a gender, its energy radiated over Gaia's body.

Rejoicing in the beauty of the third child, Gaia cried from happiness. Her salty tears filled up the large crevasses of her body, creating serpent shaped rivers as tribute to her third child's magnificence.

"You are perfection my child, as if dawn has awoken again. Where once, I lived in darkness, you are the sun that warms my skin and penetrates my heart. Is this unconditional love I feel? I shall call you Light and I will love you until I no longer exist. Carry on my legacy amongst the stars, but until then you must stay close to me, until I am sure you will not disappoint me as your brother and sister have."

Considering itself as an only child, Light lived happily on Gaia's body, cradling in the warmth of her smothering love. Light avoided contact with the humans and Witches preferring to interact with the animals that also lived on Gaia's body, particularly the dragons and unicorns, and the aliens that visited, but eventually curiosity consumed Light.

Fixated, Light studied the humans and the Witches for signs of weakness and there were many.

"What simple creatures you are but still you are glorious in your retardation."

Day became night and night became years. Light's fascination became obsession, jealousy and envy. Light wanted to be the only child of the great Gaia and the only intellect to eat and drink upon her skin.

Unable to break the obsession, Light planned to kill the humans and the Witches by merging all the rivers to drown them.

"I want to be your only child that lives upon your body."

Gaia angered, "You are unrecognisable to me, Light. Lost in your jealousy you have lost touch with your true essence. I curse you to live for an eternity in the shadows; sunlight will burn your skin and ugly your features. Your offspring are condemned to live within the disappointment of my heart, never to feel soil beneath their feet or wind upon their faces. I had given you unconditional love but you chose to worship envy instead. You will now be known as the Darkness for you have disappointed me the most."

Opening her mouth, Gaia swallowed the Darkness. Gaia felt a wave of nausea wash over her as the Darkness entered her stomach and a tiredness that heavied her eyes until she fell into a slumber.

SECRET 1
The Original Coven
Mesopotamia, c.a.4000 B.C approx.

Witches ruled the Earth. They called the Earth, Gaia- the Great Grandmother. Day or night, the Witches were the heartbeat of the Earth, the guardians of nature, the keepers of the secrets, and the wisdom that kept the Earth in balance. They were the worshippers of the soil and cleansers of the air. They produced fire from their palms for warmth, and rejuvenated the water to drink. They worked in harmony with all the elements to provide life and they did not fear their enemy- the Darkness. They abided by the lore of their mother- the Goddess, and up until today, they had not broken her trust.

Like the rumble of an earthquake before impact, the animals sensed the Original Coven flying towards them long before the Witch's leathery soles touched the sandy ground. Sensing a foreboding, some of the animals hid before the Witches' dialogue reached their alerted ears. Crawling into burrows already occupied, some were attacked and killed by the occupants while others cuddled in the safety with the dangerous predators. Frenzied, the other animals spun in circles- leaping and biting themselves. Then they turned on each other, tearing skin from the bones of the weaker opponent. Blood decorated the foliage. Although the Original Coven were protectors of all animals, tonight their presence created madness and mayhem. Menace, blanketed the air like a repellant.

Flying swiftly, arms tucked into the arches of their torso, heads facing upwards so that the moon's reflection glistened on their forehead; toes stretched, the Original Coven flew towards their chosen spot- the perfect location for such an ostentatious 'circle ritual' to cast a spell that would change the ancient world forever. Tonight under a blood moon, the Original Coven- although many times reincarnated- would cast a spell that not only would God 'their uncle' witness from Heaven (Gaia's mind), and the Darkness feel below the ground (Gaia's stomach), but would light up the night sky for the universe and the godlings (God's offspring) to observe.

The clouds cleared as the wind arrived with the thirteen Witches only minutes behind it. The gloriousness of the evening draped over them like a baby blanket. Their desire was to secure the safety of their own home by creating a protective white light around the Earth. Gaia was under threat from visitors from the stars, and the Witches were not about to allow these unwanted guest to stay, or in fact visit again.

The godlings had started worshipping these aliens from the sky, painting their image on cave walls, and worshipping them in the sunlight. These aliens had red hair and had their own magic. Contact with the aliens meant the godlings were evolving more quickly, which in turn was lessening the Witches esteem. Witches controlled the sky, not these red haired men. The Egyptians had named the aliens 'Sun Gods,' and started to worship them as new and better gods than the Witches. Even one named Ra had remained to govern. Fiercely, territorial the Witches were not about to allow aliens to conquer Gaia.

The Original Coven stood on the banks of the River Euphrates in Mesopotamia; Kali, Mary, Sophia, Ishtar, Hathor, Tara, Lilith, Isis, Fatima, Orisha, Maman Brigitte, Abonde and Circe were all celebrated as feminine divine figureheads who could with one hand pointing towards the sky command a thousand godlings into submission. Unlike God, Witches were of flesh; tangible, powerful, and Magickal and had up to now never been questioned as a just and wise authority. There was not a man who would not bow down to the Witches out of respect, or any woman who did not envy the empowerment that the Original Coven demanded. Unlike their God, the godlings could, if they dared, touch the Original Coven with the tips of their fingers and feel an eternity of truth and a holiness worthy of total loyalty.

In the beginning the Original Coven were the mightiest of Covens and their combined Magick was unstoppable. Defeating an attack on the eve of a cold and blistery Winter Solstice, the Witches had thwarted the well-fed and angry Darkness, and banished it back into the acid-filled stomach of Gaia.

On flying to the chosen spot, the Original Coven had taken a baby from a twelve year old mother who had been forced to lay with a man three times her age. The very young mother had watched as Orisha picked the baby up, tucking it into her arms. Instead of feeling the devastation of the moment, the mother had smiled and whispered, "Thank you," as the Witches flew into the night sky, and the sound of the crying baby was no more, nor was her shame or her entrapment.

Contentedly, the baby now suckled at Orisha's finger.

The Original Coven's electric green eyes, ablaze with determination scanned the landscape, without the need of speech they telepathically congratulated each other for their choice of location. The air was thinner, heightened, and savage. The water was untamed, rapid and icy cold, and would make a perfect source of channeling energy. The depth of the river indicated a recent flood which only added to the energy they could tap into.

Circe glided her hand over the river Euphrates to feel the vibrational pulse of the rapids. The river was glistening from the full moon's light- a million golden dancing stars reflected the night sky.

The river smelt of Gaia's tears, and as the godlings grew in population the pollution in the water increased.

Wars were fought and illness spread, Gaia was in desperate need of detoxifying.

Circe focused all of her thoughts on sending a powerful message to the Darkness which lurked amongst the lush green foliage that surrounded the Witches. The Darkness' eyes were like endless pits- dark and empty of life that illuminated like two yellow slits in the depths of the foliage. Although the Darkness was a prisoner of Gaia's stomach, deep within the soil, the Darkness could slip through gaps that held negativity. It saw everything that the Witches did within the blackness of the night. The Darkness was like a shadow, always present, always attached, always waiting.

Placing both palms towards each other, her long muscular fingers pointing towards the night sky, Circe manifested her Magick until it formed a glowing purple orb between her hands as large as her head. Then slowly, and with great concentration she placed the orb upon the river before letting it go. Floating, the orb lit up the river and all the surrounding area.

Circe then glided her palm over the water again, creating a constellation of stars upon the river. The stars, bright and golden, formed a pregnant divine feminine, a perfect Witch made in their image. Then she swooped her palm above the head and manifested a twelve star crown to represent the other members of the Coven. The feminine figure glowed like the sun to represent daylight Magick. Then Circe placed the moon underneath the feet to represent night-time Magick. The image of the divine feminine was a message to God and the Darkness that the Goddess sat at the top of the holy triad, and *they* made the two points at the bottom.

The whispering tongues of the Witches floated above the potential anarchy of the evening. Their intent was to commune with the elements; air, fire, water and earth. They hoped to send a message of strength and love to the Goddesses, who they missed terribly. They craved the unconditional love that only a mother can offer.

They would move like the wind, dance like the sun and worship under the moon into the early morning. They were the Original Coven, all consumed, all connected. Their spell would attune to every Witch on the earth, and it would frighten every unfaithful, 'alien loving' godling, while sending a clear and direct warning to the aliens.

Fatima noticed a wounded goat laying limp on the grass. Bending down, she placed her palm on its head and within seconds the infected cuts closed over. Healed, the goat jumped to its feet and bounded away.

Pan, the horned-deity created by Gaia to protect nature, who is everywhere but nowhere, grinned, for he was a lover of the Witches and he could feel the abundance of love the Witches had for nature. He understood a Witches' desire for equilibrium, and to protect Gaia while she slept. Teeth exposed, eyes wide, horns icy, he galloped wistfully through the forest towards them, only to stop occasionally to sniff the air, pick up their scent, puff out his chest, and sprint towards them again.

With a flick of the wrist, Kali ignited a fire. Wild and untamed, the flames travelled in a clockwise direction, jumping over the river, curving, jumping the river again, and finally joining up to form a burning protection circle around them. From the sky, it looked like a large burning eye, an 'all-seeing eye', and the Original Coven safe within it.

Scorched, the Darkness slithered backwards, stopping within the blackest crevices of the surrounding mountains. The more adventurous, inquisitive, and bravest of the Darkness returned to the edge of the fire and watched. The Witches felt the Darkness' cold stare but ignored its voyeuristic tendencies, after all, sight was its only vice in this situation, and the light from the fire was a hindrance to its capabilities.

Using two fingers, eleven of the Witches placed their fingers between the lips of their vaginas and wiped the menstruating blood across their faces. Starting from their left ear, they wiped across their cheekbone, over the sharpness of their noses, over the right cheekbone, and ended at the other ear. The blood symbolised the feminine wholeness, the cycle of the moon, and their interconnectedness. Their full moon menstruation was evidence of their feminine synchronicity. The other two Witches were pregnant.

Except for different shaped faces, and height, the Original Coven looked identical; after all, they were the purist. Made from the Goddess when she was whole, before Gaia quartered her and threw her into the four quarters of the earth as punishment for her behaviour. Thin black leather straps decorated their wrists, biceps and ankles, and a belt emphasised their large hips, but otherwise they were naked. Only their brittle and uncombed black hair warmed their bronzed skin.

Jumping on the spot, as if they were warming up to run a long distance, in unison, placing one hand over their mouths, they released a high pitched zaghareet squeal to raise the frequency of the energy that surrounded them. Like a loud trilling war cry the ululation carried across the barren landscape, and beyond the forest, waking the villagers that slept by the bank of the river.

As if suddenly pierced by an athame, the Darkness fled again, screaming into the underground where it had come from.

Animatedly, Pan arrived, sweaty faced with a flute in hand, which he placed over his whiskery lips and began to dance around the outside of the fire in a clockwise direction. Immersed in joyous rhythm, he quickly fell into a musical trance.

Maman-Brigitte, palms facing the ground, released her Magick, manifesting a flock of black roosters. Running in all directions, the roosters protected the outside of the circle as well. Scattering in all directions, the roosters ran across Pan's path, tripping him up but supple on his hooves he twirled around them with ease. Within minutes the roosters pecked any negative energy away from the ground.

Ishtar materialised a staff that was decorated with eight pointed crystal stars. Thumping it on the ground, her Magick shot out of her palm and down the staff into the soil. She did this five times. Five large and ferocious lions appeared. Eager to explore, the lions paced around the inside of the circle and then in unison, roared. Had a godling stood within a body length of the giant predators, blood would have seeped from their ears and urine from their bladders, but the Witches did not flinch as they were more frightening than any lion. Then as if highly alert, the lions, muscular and aroused, circled the Witches in a protective weave. Sensing the importance of their ritual, their manes brushed against the Witches' torsos as they circled within the inflamed compound.

Growing two more arms from her torso, Kali danced around the circle. Her eyes reflected red from the fire. Weaving around the Coven, her arms moved as if they were serpents. From her palms she sprinkled upon the ground odourless white rock salts, previously collected from the Himalayan Mountains. Within seconds the rock salt transformed into a mass of black snakes that hissed and coiled around each other. Heads hovering at shin height, the snakes struck each other in a venomous display of defense, but in awe of the Witches and lions, they moved out of their way when they sensed their feet approach, only to erupt into fury again, striking the closest snake beside them. There is no loyalty among snakes.

Then, as if Gaia knew the importance of the ritual, the breeze settled and an eerie silence greeted them. Pan stopped dancing and as if he was a child, sat down, crossed his hairy legs and placed his pan flute beside him and watched. The roosters stopped pecking and nested. The fire dimmed. The lions rested and the snakes curled around each other until they slept.

Lilith pointed her palm towards the middle of the circle. Two pink orbs released from her palms and landed in the middle, creating a very large ceramic incantation bowl which was big enough to sit four babies with ease.

Fatima started the chant, "Goddess Mother hear us now, upon the wind, join us, for our devoutness is about to sin." Then she walked over to the incantation bowl and affirmed 'good-will and intention' by blowing her breath, slow and steady into the bowl.

While the rest of the Coven continued to chant, Sophie, who was the wisest of the Coven, raised her right hand and using her index finger Magickally wrote the spell on the inside of the pottery. Starting from the centre, she twirled her finger around until it filled up with Ancient Witch symbols that circled the bowl until they reached the top.

Previously Sophie had written an Ancient Doctrine upon a clay tablet. Although they planned for success, wisdom suggested that she record their herstory (history) in case of an unexpected outcome. The tablet was safe at home.

Abonde, cupping her hands together produced the fruit of knowledge in the palms of her hands. Placing five 'cut up' apples to promote fertility and abundance- previously collected in the east- into the bowl to expose the seeded pentagram, she then poured red wine on top of it by holding her palms over the incantation bowl and wiggling her fingers. Before returning to her spot, she dipped her little finger into the red wine and tasted it. The wine was tangy.

Circe sprinkled the herbs which she kept dry in a leather pouch that was plaited in her hair, over the apples and wine. She used the herb burdock to launch an attack on their enemies, amaranth to call upon the Goddesses, ague weed and angelica for protection, anise to rise the vibration, camphor to cleanse and banish, and satin walnut to increase the potency of the other herbs. She then dripped from a ceramic jar 'dragon's blood,' covering the herbs.

Bending down, her chin almost touching her knees, Isis pushed her left hand through the snakes and placed her palm flat on the ground, while the other hand she aimed at the night sky. This was how she called her familiar, the falcon. Its screech was heard long before the glorious bird flew high about them, and its tapered wings swiftly gliding through the air. The falcon had felt the call of his mistress travel under the ground like a shockwave. Obediently, he had flown to her. The familiar was always close. Isis allowed her familiar its freedom as she was opposed to curtailing the bird from its natural disposition. A bird must fly. It must be free. Held in his beak was a polished cow horn. Mindful of the flames and the lions within the circle, the falcon dropped the cow horn into the incantation bowl and then flew back up to the safety of the night sky.

Mary looked down at her pregnant belly. The Maiden was ready to be born. Her little feet were kicking fearlessly and her body had rearranged itself two weeks earlier. It had never happened before, a Coven member falling pregnant, out of sync from the Spring Equinox and the rest of the Coven. She believed *this* Maiden was Chosen. The Coven had decided the miraculous conception was a sign that it was time to place their plans into action.

Nine months pregnant as well, Hathor the tallest Witch of the Coven had procreated with an Atlantean male. She had grown fond of the tall, white cloaked, exceedingly intelligent, higher level male energy from Atlantis, who spoke to her often about the wonders of Gaia. As the sun set they declared their love for each other and vowed to birth a Witch and Atlantean as a super race. He had laid with her for four days and nights until they were sure the seed had been planted and she was pregnant. Hathor was the first Witch to lay with a godling to create a baby. Prior, all pregnancies were from Virgin Creation which saw all the Coven pregnant at the same time. The act of sex was purely for pleasure, exercise, or to produce Sex Magick. Hathor had felt the impregnation on the first evening as the moon rose but she was not going to forgo the intimacy that was guaranteed in the union for the next three days, for her Atlantean lover's skin hummed underneath her fingertips, making her feel enlightened in his presence. Flying from the tent, she had felt woozy.

The child had grown quickly within her womb but its masculine energy had made her feel unwell. Morning sickness had kept her confined to a hammock. The child felt foreign and unnatural. She had tried to love the baby within her womb, but felt it was an abomination to the Goddesses. It was the first time a Witch carried a male baby. It should have been the last.

Eager to start the ritual, Orisha laid the sleeping godling baby into the incantation bowl and returned to her position.

Mary stood beside the incantation bowl for a long time contemplating the next step and although the baby within her belly was a Maiden, she knew that the baby's Magick- even though not Awakened- was important for the success of the spell, and it was important that she remained loyal to *her* Coven. Placing both palms on her belly, her skin tore apart, and once she could slide her hands inside her stomach she grabbed the Maiden out. Holding her upside down, Mary tapped the Maiden's fleshy bum and without effort, the Maiden cried. A perfect newborn, she already had thick black hair, green potent eyes and perfect pouty lips. The umbilical fluid washed into the bowl. Quickly allowing the Maiden a feed from her swollen breasts, she then calmly placed the baby into the incantation bowl. Larger than the godling baby by at least a heads length, she took up more of the space. Instantly sucking her thumb, the Maiden settled into a deep sleep.

Lastly Hathor- who was eager to see what her masculine child looked like- repeated the same technique as Mary. The baby came out as if he already had a strong spine and neck. The newborn was as tall as the Maiden but his skin was pasty and white and his eyes were transcending blue. She did not feed him.

With the three babies now all asleep within the bowl, Orisha produced a small bottle from the leather belt she wore. Untying the fabric from the top, she poured the sticky liquid contents (semen, blood and urine) into the palm of her hand. With the tip of her finger she wrote the number six on each baby's forehead. The number six represented Gaia and all things important to the Coven; harmony, love, family, and motherhood. But what they did not acknowledge was their unspoken grief from losing their own mother an eternity ago, and the trauma it had caused them watching her torn into quarters. It tainted the number six with resentment, fear and anger. For those who love must also feel pain. It was a truth, and although what they felt was morally right and just, within this spell, it polluted the good-will. Before they even began the spell was tainted.

Now they would wait.

It would not be long before the moon turned coppery red as if bleeding. A lunar eclipse meant that their Magick would be potent. The earth, sun and moon would align. The moon would go through all the stages of a lunar cycle: a full moon, waxing, waning and finish again as a full moon within hours of performing the spell, reaching every quarter of the earth with accuracy and strength beyond any spell ever performed. The Witches wanted the universe to feel the energy wave.

The danger lay not with the colour of the moon but with the night sky which would be at its blackest, leaving the Witches potentially vulnerable to the Darkness. The hope was that the fire, lions, snakes and roosters would protect them, as it was important not to be disturbed while casting the spell.

Sensing it would not be long before the lunar eclipse began; one by one, they all scooped up the liquid in the incantation bowl with the cow horn and took turns drinking from it before chanting, "Together we drink, together we are one."

The Witches ignored the babies' whimpers and tears.

It was time to cast the spell.

Firstly, they had to summon their mother, the Goddess.

Isis faced east and marched over to the flames. The snakes hissed and then settled as she passed. As the flames warmed her skin, she felt one of the lions stand beside her. Raising her hands high above her, she released a yellow stream of Magick into the sky. As if she was commanding an army of a thousand people, she yelled, "Wake from your slumber, oh mother, and come to our aid, as fast as wind, blow our way."

All together they chanted, "Mother Goddess, we welcome you!"

An angry wind arrived which blew the Witches hair across their faces. The lions roared as their manes irritated their eyes and whipped their faces. The snakes all arched and hissed. Pan cackled, and the roosters pecked.

Lilith was already facing south with a lion already standing beside her. Raising her hands the colour red shot from her palms into the sky and with a deep voice, she commanded the fire, "Wake from your slumber, oh mother, and come to our aid, as fast as fire, burn our way."

All together they chanted, "Mother Goddess, we welcome you!"

The fiery circle grew twice its height as she arrived. Any chill within the circle was soon gone.

Ishtar stood slightly back from the fire due to being worried that her beloved lions might get scorched by the unpredictable flames. On either side a lion protected their mistress. Curiously, both stared west into the flames as if they could see something sinister. Raising her hands, a blue stream left her palms and shot into the sky. With a higher pitched voice than the others, she commanded the appearance of her mother, "Wake from your slumber, oh mother, and come to our aid, as cleansing as water, purify our way."

All together they chanted, "Mother Goddess, we welcome you!"

A clash of thunder assured she had heard, and within seconds it started to rain outside of the circle.

Mary took a look at her daughter in the incantation bowl before walking north. Raising her hands, the colour green shot into the sky. "Wake from your slumber, oh mother, and come to our aid, as grounding as soil, steady our way."

All together they chanted, "Mother Goddess, we welcome you!"

All four colours; yellow, red, blue and green connected high above them forming a pyramid. The last quarter of the Goddess appeared more kindly this time by simply moving the soil beneath their feet which tickled their toes.

Now the quarters were joined, their mother was whole again and as close to them as possible. They felt her love and the warmth of her heart beating within the circle. Safe now that she had arrived, they continued.

All thirteen Witches walked towards the incantation bowl.

Isis, Lilith, and Ishtar Magickally produced their athames, and held them high above their heads. Then with cold-hearted conviction, they brought the ritual blade down and cut the babies heads off.

As the incantation bowl filled with blood, the thirteen Witches soaked their hands in it. They then locked hands forming a powerful alliance. Arching their backs, their arms stretched out, they began to dance in a clockwise direction.

Their chants got louder each full lap of the circle, "Heee hum ah, heee hum ah, hee hum ah, huma hee."

Safe within the fiery circle and the pyramid their Magick- like steam- evaporated off their warm skin, and in an upward spiral, Magickically orbited until it reached the top of the pyramid and channelled through the small peak, exploding with such force that the earth shook. Interrupting the frequency of the earth, millions of birds lost their senses and fell out of the sky, dying on impact with the ground.

Frightened, the godlings ran out of their homes and watched as a bright white serpent, like a comet flew across the sky in four directions. Then it flew at tremendous speed, clockwise across the earth, circling repeatedly, covering Gaia in a white blanket.

Channelling their Magick with such intensity, jagged and twisted in motion, their bodies moved faster, until at times their bodies disappeared and they entered the realm of the Goddesses, just long enough to see their mother and enter the physical realm again.

Chanting became hissing and their jagged movement became sweeping, and their commands became enchantments.

Trees all over the earth started to twist around themselves, oceans sunk a little and the weather angered.

The moon was coppery red now. The lunar eclipse was at its most potent. The spell was working. A layer of white light was almost complete around the earth. The protective circle would stop the aliens flying through it in their silvery spacecraft.

Witches all over the world raised their palms towards the sky and connected to the stream. It was the most glorious sight imaginable. Black and white were one. All Witches were connected.

Determined to see their mother again, the Original Coven danced faster and wilder, but as happiness consumed them, what they saw shattered their confidence. Their mother was crying and pointing behind the Coven to the west.

Unprepared for such an image, they foolishly let go of each other's hands and consequently were hurtled back into the physical realm. Their Magick stopped channeling and an eerie quietness made them shiver. The fire dimmed until it went out completely and the animals submitted to something unforeseen. Then without warning the white light disappeared from the sky and as the full moon was burning with a red halo, the earth suddenly stopped vibrating. The world was in complete darkness, except for a red glow around the moon.

Unable to see her own hands, Isis reached out to search for her Coven sisters but could not find any. All her senses were affected due to some interference.

"Hathor? Sophia? Tara?"

The sound of a high pitched squeal deafened her.

Then a biting chill, unlike any cold she had ever felt, travelled up her spine lifting the hair at the back of her head up, before the chill shivered out the top of her cranium. Before she could react, an undeniably large entity jumped onto her back, forcing her to bend at the knees and collapse onto the ground. Her hands took the brunt of the contact and then her chin. First she thought a lion had attacked her, until the accuracy of the large claws that now scratched at her forehead and cheeks changed her mind. Finally finding its target, the entity placed its claws into her eye sockets and scraped her eyeballs out. The entity then released its grip and hopped off her, not before turning her over and scratching a symbol on her forehead. It was a triangle without one line. It was an arrow-head, and it symbolised the partnership between God and the Darkness.

Releasing a scream that haunted all those who could hear it, Isis threw up from the pain. Hands frantically touching the empty, bloody sockets of her face, she released another scream- one of grief and shock. Then as suddenly as her deafness had happened, she could hear again and as if on a battle field, Isis was surrounded by thousands of voices, shrieking, yelling and crying. She could hear her Coven being slaughtered, but unable to see, she could not save them.

Unable to find the strength to stand, she crawled along the ground, tangling with the snakes that frantically slithered away from the chaos. Trying to hear where the Witches were, she listened but all she heard was screams from all directions. The Darkness had sabotaged them, and impaired her vison so she could not fight, but why had they not killed her? She had thought the Witches had protected themselves sufficiently, but now she realised they had made a huge blunder. The Darkness and God had found a way to break through the Magickal barriers, and now the Original Coven was being slaughtered.

To the left of her, she heard the sobs of Ishtar who had just found her lions dead. Their large muscular bodies limp on the ground. Their necks broken. Then, Ishtar stopped crying and was not heard of again. In fact, Isis could no longer hear any of her Coven sisters. Suddenly, she was alone, very…very alone. Trying to hear the Coven sisters filled her with dread. They were gone. She could not sense them anymore. The first time in eternity, she was without her Coven.

Unexpectedly, a high pitched ringing started in her left ear, travelled through the centre of her head, and then back out the other ear. Then as if it was a normal night, the birds started to tweet again and the river started to flow. The sound of Pan playing his flute calmed not only the animals but her as well.

Standing up slowly, Isis stumbled forwards, hands stretched out she searched for life, for a friend. The snakes' dead bodies tangled her up. It felt like days as she wandered purposely on the banks of the river, calling out to the Original Coven but there was no reply.

Scared for the first time in her existence, she sat on the bank of the river and cried.

"I'll bring you back home. I'll bring you back home," she sobbed.

Just as she contemplated drowning herself, the earth trembled with such rage that she clung for her life on the rocks.

Gaia was unbalanced.

The rivers ran red.

Frightened, the godlings ran erratically for safety, again. Their sheep-skin clothes could not protect them from the unpredictability of the weather and many perished within seconds from flying debris and stupidity.

Atlanteans that survived the first tremor, did not survive the tsunami that sunk the city off the coast half an hour later, which dragged Atlantis and their beloved bulls into the depths of the icy cold water, lost forever. Their wisdom and knowledge trapped at the bottom of the ocean.

After the destruction what remained was the image Circe had created in the river only hours before. The image without Isis knowing was now a symbol of hope, that when the same image could be seen in the sky, she would reconnect with the Original Coven again.

SECRET TWO
Queen Elizabeth 1st
(Reincarnated as Deity in S^ORD)
England, 21st of March, 1603.

"I should like to surrender. Not from the halls of contempt that sharpen men's minds. Not from the melancholy of continuous reign, or the constant heartache of betrayal and treason. Not from executions, wars, taxes, financial hardship or the steady requirement of my signature and how it pains my wrist, but simply and justly, I surrender from myself. My powdered mask has hidden my guilt and my own treason wilfully from the English. Witches should never reign over people, although I have for almost forty five years- an imposed duty due to my mother, Anne Boleyn. I was unfaithful to my post, not from matters of heart, but because my true conviction was and will always be Witchcraft and to my true self- a Witch. Witchcraft is the bed to which I sleep well at night. They can place a crown upon my head and refer to me as Queen, but I was never a true representative of God's will. There were nights that I prayed for intervention, that I crawled inside of my own skin for answers. The crown merely itched my forehead as it sat uncomfortably upon my head, as thorns sat upon Jesus. But I governed as Queen the best I could. I must admit that as I grew older, God's radiance flooded through the window more elegantly, but I never heard him mutter one word upon my ear. I should have liked to have heard his voice; the tone, the pitch, the reason, and as I stand here now, I beg him to speak to me. For sometimes I do not believe he exists. Faith is such folly. His followers have such confidence for a voice they cannot hear. They hear someone, a voice that speaks with conviction but it is not God they hear, but their own diplomacies. God must enjoy their ambitions. I have no need to devalue him, nor antagonise, but God is not my moral compass. I admit I used him for my own purposes to strengthen my position. He simply *is* and that is all that matters, so therefore I feel no guilt in my manipulation. If only they knew the truth that it was the Goddesses that I asked for guidance and leniencies as I ruled. How the court would have shuddered. It is my guilt that worries me, forever torn between my true self and my duty to England. Of course, England is home to Witches as well, and its land's preservation is important to our well-being, but who am I to choose its discourse? I have lived few reincarnations. I do not have the knowledge or wisdom for such endeavours nor the fierceness of a soldier, or the adventurous nature of a sea explorer. I am Elizabeth, daughter of Anne Boleyn- an insincere Witch, and Henry- who governed with such force he forgot he was merely a man. I do not undermine his heritage- the Red Haired Men's leader, a man who once wielded his own magic, a male magic that no longer exists in him but inside of me. And who am I to know the mind of others, for I do not know the truths of my own mind. Gaia, the one true creator has disowned us, but more disappointing is that I failed Witch-kind. Concerned with matters of state and male-polluted politics, I have spent a lifetime weaving a basket for them to decide what is to be carried within it. My largest regret is how I failed women. How women suffer? Men might die from their wounds, but women must keep breathing, and that is true strength. My mother's desire for reform will be retired soon, and they will forget me and they will continue to speak of her with distrust, for she was a disloyal Witch. I believe the suffering of women influenced my mother's decisions. It was not worthy of such extravagance, and left me trapped within Anne's poisoned breast, and it is *this* profanation that I cannot rest, that I stay awake for days unable to find comfort in any sitting positon. For our future is a 'standing position' requirement. There is no doubt my position has held privilege for Witches, not only here but in all the nations combined. Witches must live in harmony with all, the 'Blood Oath' states this very clearly. The Pope's disdain for me, his knowledge that Witches exist torments his soul and feeds his resentment into Spanish egos. It was only through my diplomatic sensibilities that my mother's interference was not the ruination of our existence. They hang innocent women, men and children for a craft they know little about. Can you imagine what they would have done had they known the truth? Our invisibility is our strength. Magick would have deterred them but how many of them do we need to murder? Shall we destroy them all? We are not monsters. Not to sound defeated, I am only sharing my thoughts to release pressure from my thoughts. I desire to join the Goddesses for a rest now, hence the reason I call you here this evening and I thank you for coming when asked. You have all honoured your position and it will be written in the White Library and remembered. I leave the people with no successor, but I cannot leave the Witches so futile. Blanche my friend and chief gentlewoman, asked me before she died what it was like to die, as if my communion with God made me privy to such matters? I wanted to share with her the truth that I was a Witch, as many suspected of my mother, but Blanche was a devout woman and to speak of such truths would have ruined her meeting with God and the comfort of her own morality. Although I have lived a selfish existence, my love for her secured the moment and I assured her that death was generous. I saw her eyes soften. It is the taking of life before its time that is unkind. As a vessel of this unkindness I am heavily burdened. Life always asks too much of me and I grow resentful. Power is a superior burden."

Elizabeth looked towards the ceiling to imagine what it must look like inside Gaia's mind.

Relieved from performing her last monologue, Elizabeth smiled. Her face was clear of make-up exposing her wrinkles. Her greyish auburn hair was piled high above her head, divorcing her from her youth, and although frail, she stood as if a pole made from conviction supported her. She had claimed vulnerability within her speech, but the Crone that stood before the Coven was nothing but a stature of integrity.

In the beginning of her reign as Highest Priestess, the Sisters of the Moon had distrusted Elizabeth. She was after all the daughter of Gorr, the last surviving male of the Red Haired Men and his Soulmate, the Witch Anne. Elizabeth, was not considered an Ancient, or a Non-Ancient and therefore her alliance was compromised and her positioned questioned, but she always spoke from her own awareness, and therefore always proved herself loyal to the Coven.

Elizabeth never claimed an allegiance to either faction, even if she had wanted to as her Magick was a mixture of Ancient (pure) and Non-Ancient (impure), and she was first born *after* the Black and Red war with her father's male Magic. Three Magickal strains vibrated within her stomach, and unlike other Witches, she was born with her Magick already Awakened. She was able to release Magick from her palms, but also wield a wand and summon male magic. She was a Witch in limbo, a mixture of disparagement that cultivated into self-contempt. Three strains of Magick fighting for superiority in one body left Elizabeth no option but to reign with *only* her mind, or otherwise allow the chaos to spill over into anarchy.

Ancients, were the original Witches. Pure and robust, they had fought the Red Haired Men- a mysterious clan who arrived by boat to conquer England. However the Red Haired Men's magic, through breeding with the Witches weakened the Witches Ancient Magick and created new Witch energies- the Non-Ancient Witch, a hybrid strain. Their Magick was weak and a sour reminder of that disastrous era.

Non-Ancients cannot produce Magick from their palms, but instead required wood from an Ancient Tree. The earthy tool is taken from the roots of the Ancient Tree through a technique called Fire Hardening. The moisture is removed from the root making the wood harden, and then with a special stone the root is polished, bringing forth the elements required for such Magick. On Awakening, the Non-Ancients remember the means to channel their Magick through a wand.

Witch-tales tell of Gorr, who fell inlove with a Maiden, and on the eve of her murder, he cut his chest open and bled upon her corpse, cursing their souls to be entwined for eternity. To his torment, he is reincarnated with the Maiden, who he cannot remember, forever her follower, not always her focus. He is fiercely attracted to her but does not know why. Had Henry known that Anne was his Soul-mate, perhaps he would not have been so eager to cut off her head. Elizabeth could only imagine his outrage that she had betrayed him. It had been his eternal love for her that forced his signature upon the paper that warranted her execution. The pain of love, stronger than hate, was the true prerequisite for wishing her dead.

Facing the Sisters of the Moon, who had listened intently to their sixty nine year old Highest Priestess' speech, Elizabeth coiled within their respect of her.

Twelve Ancient Crones had watched Elizabeth live two lives in one reincarnation, and if she chose to die now, than who were they to deny her such a liberty? Surely, the Goddesses would allow her this privilege?

"The reason I called you to Coven is that I wish to deter such happenings again. I cannot allow my life to have been for vanity, for pride does not suit me. I bring forth a proposal, swift and unforgiving. With power comes great accountability, and today I must make another decision. We are thinkers before action. We are wisdom before swords. Let us create a future of boundless possibilities. Let us remove our garments and cloaks. If only all great decisions were made while naked."

It was a novelty to undress herself without the fuss of her chamber maids. Her title of Queen stripped her of her basic rights. It was a pleasure to undress in front of the Coven as an empowered feminine energy. Nudity was a Witches preferred twilight gown. With the unbuttoning and dropping of the garments upon the floor, designed to symbolise her oneness with Gaia, she still noticed a desire to hide behind the fabric, a safety she had become accustomed to, and at times during her latest reincarnation, especially when the cold weather set into her bones, she favoured.

She pulled the ribbons of her corset and enjoyed the drop of her breasts. If Magick could be compared, it would be equated to the releasing of the restriction of the breasts.

"Please sit down. I apologise for the inadequate space on the rug and the humbleness of the floor but let us pretend that we are supple in our age."

The queen's chamber was damp, and the chill soon lashed their flabby skin, but they were relieved to have permission to rest their aching bodies upon the thick red rectangle rug that had been placed perfectly in the middle of the room to allow ample walking space around its parametres.

Seven pillows were thrown haphazardly across the rug in an unsubtle attempt to persuade rest. Two large candelabras in adjacent corners of the stone walls stood with lit candles to flicker light across the room. A large window decorated with heavy white curtains had been draped back to expose a starry night, absent of the moon. The other two large windows facing each other, east to west, were uncovered, exposing London's seedy character, and if one was to look through the west window towards the river Thames, they would have witnessed a haunting vision on such an uneasy night of a mist floating with the current.

"Let us not worry ourselves with rituals tonight but speak instead of morality."

A guard of Richmond Palace, unaware of the Queen's reasons, protected the room from nosy residents who may claim the right to open the door and accidently discover the Queen's true identity on the eve of her death.

Her chambermaids, although not privy to the Queen's true identity, were competent in secrecy. Jealous however, they sat around the fire gossiping about what was happening behind the solid locked door. They had on many occasions glimpsed the arrival of the cloaked women, whose arrivals were always sudden and late at night, but none had ever been close enough to see their faces hidden underneath the heaviness of their hoods.

Once settled upon the rug, the Crones remained faithful to their Highest Priestess by remaining silent. Their words rested on their tongues. They only allowed their eyes to speak.

"I would like to speak once more without interruption, to repeat a story I heard from a traveller, and you will muse at its forecast. I wonder if somehow Plato had heard the story of my mother and father. I believe all great stories are based on truth, swirled around in a pot, and spoon-fed to the captured audience. Storytellers are scandalous troublemakers, scorned with ink and paper, or the gift of speech. They are more treacherous than the Privy Council as they mask their opinions in humour and tragedy. I should have had them all hanged had I not enjoyed their antics. Had I had a lover to keep me warm at night, perhaps I would not have fancied in the Arts as much as I did. The story in which I tell you tonight is one of warning. I am a logical Witch, and I announced this to the traveller, but I enjoyed his storytelling. Bathing a month later, I was still consumed with his story and believed the Goddesses had brought him to me on purpose. The story he repeated was 'Symposium' which is told by Aristophane, an Ancient Athenian comic playwright and it tells of the first people, whose appearance would frighten most. Born with four arms and legs, two faces and two sets of sexual organs, both of female and male, this hideous creature is named, man, woman and androgynous. This is where it intrigues me, because up until now the story is, I surmise, only to scare children. The story suggests that, man is from the sun and woman is from the earth and the children are from the Moon. In the beginning the story explains that the original people threaten to challenge the Gods, and in retaliation, the Gods tear the first people in half, and they are then forever saddened in their new form. Forever looking for their other half. My father was from the sun and my mother from the earth and I am always chosen by the Goddesses to represent the moon. Imagine how I sat back on my chair after hearing such a story? Were the Goddesses forewarning me that if my mother and father continue to challenge God, there will be retribution for us all? The story continues in greater detail then I have spoken of today, and I am corrupted with subjectivity, however, the essence of truth worried me. Had Plato heard of the Black and Red War? If only I could sit with the man and contest his mind. A man who writes of great love surely would have been obsessed with the story of my mother and father. So I concluded, although it has always been *our* way to protect our Innocent Maidens under the spell of Obscurity until they are Awaken, perhaps it is time we did not? My mother and father are too dangerous, even in whisper, to have such an advantage each reincarnation. Tonight, we must decide to change a Witch Lore and remove their anonymity before their next birth. We cannot allow them to share in powers beyond their rights. To allow them, once again, to challenge the will of the Goddesses and God. I am only asking to limit her birthright. We must agree tonight. Losing her head does not deter her. All I ask is that you consider this course, and believe it is the will of the Goddesses."

Elizabeth waited for a response. Looking around the room she studied the expressions of the Crones, but found no comfort in their stares. A cough alerted her that someone was about to speak. She braced herself for the reaction.

Essie spoke, "You speak on behalf of our Goddesses now High Priestess because you are accustomed to speaking on behalf of God? What if you are wrong and it is the will of man that you ask us to mutilate the most powerful Witches Rite, the lore of Obscurity? The Witch Lore is there to protect us from our own retribution until we are Awakened and able to defend ourselves. It has always been this way."

Taken back by Essie's harshness of tone, Elizabeth reminded herself that she had expected and prepared herself for opposition.

"I am only asking to restrict the protection of Obscurity to protect *all* the Witches from her ambitions. I am not asking you to take her Magick. Need I remind you all, that it was not that long ago that her own Coven, the last Sisters of the Moon who inhibited her Magick, leading to her downfall, and three years later saw her head removed from her body, again? Her own Coven made the difficult decision of curtailing her ambitious nature and now will be subjected to punishment by the Goddesses for backstabbing one of their own Coven sisters and surely will not all be reincarnated together next time. Only those who did not betray Anne will be reborn with her. I am not asking you to suppress her Magick. But you will be accountable for her misgivings. I pray in my sensibilities that this is the right decision."

"Witches do not *pray*, Highest Priestess! Witches commune. You have spent too long in the 'glory' of God," Essie snapped.

A quieter voice spoke, "Do you truly believe that your mother and father are capable of challenging God and potentially the Goddesses? The story is just a story, perhaps and you are tired and paranoid?"

Elizabeth bowed her head, tightness in the back of her neck caused an abrupt stop, short of its desired spot, and as if in prayer, she closed her eyes. Moments later, after she had listened to her inner voice, she replied, "I am born a Witch not a Maiden. I am the only one of my kind. I am Awakened from my first breath, and therefore, I cannot sympathise with you on the importance of Obscurity Lore, however I am plagued with memory, as distorted as they appear without reprise and therefore, perhaps this is why I was told the story and why I find its meaning powerful. I was born for a reason, perhaps to hamper the determinations of my mother and father. To answer your question, I believe my mother is capable of any measure that she fancies. This is my dying wish. I want to be reincarnated to a better world. I plead, quieten your minds and seek the answer."

In a jagged circle on the rug the Sisters of the Moon held hands, closed their eyes and drew strength from their Coven. After several minutes, their shuffling and rearranging of sitting positions alerted Elizabeth that they were ready to vote.

It would be the last time Elizabeth would sit with the Crones and it saddened her.

"Before we vote, I want to thank you for your companionship and for your acceptance of my authority. Chosen by the Goddesses to unite our Magick, we have become one. I believe, we have been to date, the most productive and harmonious Coven, and will always be remembered and spoken of highly."

Smiles emerged from the Crones for the first time that evening and a softening of heart that reminded them of their love for each other. They had a close bond. Perhaps their Highest Priestess was right, after all she had governed wisely.

With one united gesture all thirteen Crones lifted their arms and turned their hands upright to expose their palms. They had all chosen 'reason'. Anne was to be suppressed- they would remove the Obscurity Spell. Witches would know of her heritage the moment she was born. As a Maiden, her potential would be curtailed.

A relieved giggle escaped Elizabeth's mouth. She was betraying her own mother but knew that she was securing the well-being of *all*

Witches. It was a motion supported by logic and not faith. If she had learned one thing, it was to put her faith into reason.

Tired of endless ritual preparation they cast the circle by placing their cloaks in a circle around them. They did not ask the Goddesses to join them.

Placing their palms to the front of them, facing the middle of the room, the Crones released a stream of Magick from their palms that connected and spiraled upwards. Purple, blue, green, yellow, orange, and red spun like a tornado towards the ceiling. Its cloud-like appearance burst into thousands of silver stars that instantly formed cogs from a clock. Ancient symbols circled the clock face. The larger hand of the clock ticked anti-clockwise, quickening as it spun until it was moving so fast it disappeared. The gustiness of the Magick blew the candles out, threw the pillows against the four walls and lifted the Crones' hair so high it looked as if they were hanging upside down.

Elizabeth shouted, "In the beginning, Gaia created the Earth, in merry may, its integrity mirth. From Goddesses to Witches, we witnessed her birth, a feeble child in Magickal girth. However through the years, gained an ego worth. And although it pains us to control her Berth, blessed be, I denounce her. As we are one, it shall no longer be, for she must be measured and it's agreed. On this date, under the moon 1603, we take away the spell Obscurity. And although it pains us to control her Berth, blessed be, I denounce her."

As if the room was subject to an internal earthquake, the backdraft from the Magick consumed itself and vanished into a black hole. The pillows fell to the floor and the candles re-lit. The Crones' hair gently rested on their tight shoulders, and as if they were unsure of what they had done it took several seconds for their palms to re-join their sides.

Relieved but ashamed of her own betrayal, Elizabeth cried. It was the only time she had ever shown a vulnerable side to the Sisters of the Moon. It was only when she was alone with the Goddesses that she allowed herself the admit acknowledgement that she was weak at times.

Elizabeth dismissed her guard before saying goodbye to each Crone individually. After their farewells and good wishes she settled in for another night in her chamber with no food or water and only one candle lit to distract her from the pains in her body. She suspected the ceruse paste made from white lead and vinegar that she wore upon her face, neck and chest was making her greyish and pox like. She had a strong belief that the healthiness of one's skin was a mirror to the internal health of the body. In her noble vanity, she was killing herself and happily so. If the paste was indeed poison like her doctor's warned, than she would wear it even thicker. She had not asked the Witches to make their potions to heal her, she had wanted an early retirement.

Elizabeth questioned the heaviness of her chest. She had wanted resolution but even now as the spell was cast and her mother curtailed, she could not settle.

Walking to the western window, she acknowledged that the soles of her feet hurt, particularly in the arches. She desired a foot massage, or someone to rub her back, but at what cost? Intimacy had always come at a price for her.

The sound of creaking near the door interrupted her thinking. She turned to face a dark figure standing in front of the closed doorway.

"May I ask who is standing in front of me, uninvited and hidden within the darkness?"

Elizabeth noticed its body was hunched over as if it had carried large barrels of French white wine at the docks. A large piece of fabric made from hessian which could easily envelope an elephant had been loosely wrapped around it several times, finally secured over its right shoulder and tied together under its left armpit.

Looking directly at her, its silence directed her to its insolence.

Elizabeth felt threatened from its sheer size, but she had waited for this moment her entire life.

She demanded a response, "Who are you?"

"I have come."

"I asked for God, I doubt *you* are anyone's god."

Laughter from the back of its throat, deep and monotone, oozed the smell of week old rubbish into the air.

Elizabeth fought the urge to vomit as its stench reached each corner of the chamber.

What intrigued Elizabeth was the overlapping of laughter that echoed around the room, bouncing off the walls like a ball and landing at her feet.

She stepped closer to the stranger, "Am I to fear you, for it is you that hides in the darkness, not me?"

With contempt the stranger stepped closer. The thud of its step buckled the floorboard and it was only from the wood's strength that it withstood the weight.

"I watched you cast the spell. I stood in this corner. Your Coven did not even sense my presence and I heard every word you spoke. I know what you have done Witch. You have made a great blunder tonight Elizabeth, for I added a clause to the spell."

Elizabeth's breathe quickened. Her skin cooled as her head heated. In that moment, she realised that she had ignored the one rule that must never be overlooked when casting a spell- always protect the circle. After several lifetimes of gaining acceptance she had failed her Coven. On the eve of her death she had made the greatest mistake of her existence- she had been lazy and complacent, safe in an illusion of power. She had sense an easiness in her final days which ironically was to her detriment.

Deciding to challenge the stranger she used dismissiveness, a projection of power that she so desperately needed at that very moment, "I think, I shall like to go to bed now. So speak of your purpose or leave. I have better things to do with my time."

It walked towards her, each step slow but steady, demanding attention as the floorboards buckled underneath. It stopped a footstep away from her and stared into her eyes as if it was trying to burn them.

It was then that Elizabeth realised that the stranger had two faces and four black pits for eyes.

Elizabeth stepped backwards towards the window.

"Why do you come to me with two faces?"

"Because you are two faced."

The stranger cupped Elizabeth's chin and moved her face from right to left, as if it was deciding which profile it preferred or which side of her face to smash in. Then another hand grabbed her around the neck, squeezing it just tight enough to frighten her. Then as if it was playing with her, a third hand cupped her breast. But just as it lifted its' fourth hand, Elizabeth grabbed it and forced it into its chest, "Tell me what have you done?"

"It has been foretold that the Darkness will return when a Non-Ancient rules and your mother's Magick is burned from the pit of her stomach. God will be released from Gaia's mind. The ejected souls from heaven are ours to feast upon. At night, we will enter in our thousands devouring flesh from the bones of those who live. They are only food to us though, it's the Witches we want. Your Magick will allow us to return to the sunlight."

Why tell me? You're either arrogant or stupid?"

Angering, the stranger unravelled its clothed wrap, uncoiling from it like a snake from its skin, exposing its hideous appearance. Two stocky legs stabilised its balance, while the other two thinner legs linked behind its bottom to make a large bulge. Swiftly, it released the two thinner legs to join the other two.

Elizabeth cursed herself for dismissing the guard who would have surely returned with help by now.

She retaliated again, "Your prophesy is just a story."

The stranger smiled, "It isn't now. We sent you the storyteller and like a fool, you did exactly as we planned. Three Magick Witch!"

In her ignorance, she never imagined the storyteller had known she was a Witch.

Monstrous in its form, the Darkness did not scare her, for there had been another narrator in her life- her mother. Anne, had left a written letter of her dealings with the Darkness, of the mighty battle where the Darkness had been defeated by the Witches and thrown back into the depths of Gaia's stomach.

The hideous stranger did not have time to react before Elizabeth placed both of her hands inside each of its mouth and ripped out both of its tongues, flinging the tongues across the room.

The moment of surprise gave Elizabeth the advantage and she grabbed the Darkness by its left neck and ran across the room, smashing it into the stone wall. Part of the stone wall broke away creating a storm of shards that became missiles across the room.

"Do you feel my strength Darkness? You will not break me. You will not even make me bend. Go back home and say, Elizabeth is *born*. I am the daughter of the Earth and the Sun and the Moon. I am a triple threat. If anyone was prophesied it was ME! I will be the greatest deity even known. I am no whore's daughter. I'm coming for you. When I am born again, I will hunt the Darkness down. I will enter Gaia's stomach and destroy the Darkness. The Darkness is no equal. And I don't believe in God."

SECRET THREE
Vatican City, Italy, 1975.

Arriving in Rome only five hours before, Nicneven travelled straight to the Nunnery where she was staying, unpacked, ate, and then proceeded to the magnificence of St Peters Square which was 'where and when' she discovered it was in fact the shape of a circle.

The crowds had gathered, and although many armed men stood in the alcoves, they stole only a small amount of attention compared to the awe-inspiring monuments that seduced her eyesight every direction she looked. As if she was at a rock concert, the crowd fidgeted in anticipation of any sight of his holiness, the Pope.

Within her large handbag, she had a black veil ready to place over her head once inside the secret chambers of the Vatican. She enjoyed, if not encouraged the early morning sun burning the top of her head. Italy was a welcomed respite from the cold English weather.

Not easily spooked, she was surprised that once inside the doors of the Vatican, the haunted atmosphere made her shiver. Even for a Witch, she respected the history inside of the walls. The two thousand year old Vatican City, built on ancient burial grounds contained archives which the Vatican would happily sacrifice to protect the Ancient Doctrine. The Ancient Doctrine was the most important document ever written, kept in the White Library in London where Witches could protect it.

A young girl who clung to her father's trousers, with panicked eyes, scanned the artworks that made the walls look like a patchwork quilt and loudly boasted, "Daddy? It's like people are watching me."

Making the wrong turn, Nicneven found herself shoulder to shoulder in the middle of a flustered and tired onslaught of tourists who were forced, like cows squashed into the back of a truck destined for the slaughter house, to inch by inch, move down the stuffy halls of the Vatican.

Eventually reaching the modern double helix spiral staircase, which she knew was an architectural symbol for Feminine Energy, she shuffled downwards in a clockwise direction, avoiding contact with those walking back up and then at the bottom she exited the herd. With absolute determination, she aggressively pushed people out of her way, finally reaching the safety of the wall.

A security guard who appeared out of nowhere, checked the contents of her bag and then ushered for her to follow him.

She had declared in feminine poise, "A girl's gotta have a big bag."

Sliding quickly behind his body, she followed him to the original spiral Bramante staircase, where they exited at the second door at the bottom which lead to the Pope's private chambers.

"I will wait here," the security man demanded in a monotone speech before reminding her to place the black veil over her face before entering the Pope's chambers.

Although irritated that she had to place the black laced veil over her head to conceal her face, after all she was not in mourning, the opposite in fact, she did as she was asked.

The black veil was a reminder to the Pope that a man should fear a woman. That he had no place laying his eyes upon her face. That he should bow down to her womb.

Wearing all black attire; a knee length a-shaped dress that buttoned up to her chin, stockings to hide her pale white legs and court shoes, she only wished that she had a stereo-typical Witches hat to place on her head instead of the veil. However, she was now unrecognisable which she thought would be an advantage, however her vision was impaired which was a disadvantage.

Three knocks assured quick entrance into the room. A brief introduction occurred before she was left alone with Pope Paul VI, who sat watching a film on a television screen that was set in a hard Blackwood cabinet. The film she recognised as the Rocky Horror Picture Show.

She grinned.

Enthusiastically, the Pope converted his attention to her. Slowly standing up he walked towards her, automatically expanding his hand out, implying that she should kiss the Papal Ring, but before the awkward interaction and undoubting refusal, he pulled his hand back and spoke, "Forgive me. It is a habit now," he smiled. "Nun joke. Pun intended."

Not wanting to miss out on a juvenile jest, she replied, "I always thought it smelt a bit...fishy," referring to the legend that the Papal

Ring was originally the ring of a fisherman. Looking at the highly polished replicate on his boney finger, Nicneven doubted that the original golden ring ever touched the fingers of a fisherman, nor any commoner.

They both laughed, and then as if they both remembered why she was there they both poised.

"I was just watching 'Horror, Rocky…something like that. It is very good. Men wearing dresses. Who would have thought?"

Looking at his long robes, she responded, "Yes, who would have thought?"

As if suddenly conscious of the time, the Pope looked over her shoulder at the view of the crowd outside. Nicneven noticed his shoulders raise and his jaw clench.

"It is very lovely to meet you. To be honest, I hadn't anticipated the nerves before meeting you."

Grabbing her hand and placing it between both his palms in an intimate display of affection, he grinned, "Garnet-Ember has spoken constantly of your visit for days. She tells me it has been about a thousand years since you last saw each other?"

"Perhaps. Our timelines are often out. Until now. I am however still loyal to the cause. As I shall be for eternity. No offence, but Witches will rule the world again."

"Some Witches already do," he winked.

Staring into his eyes, she saw a kind man. His eyebrows were bushy as if he was a man in his thirties, although his arched back and wobbly knees highlighted his true age.

Nicneven looked at him intently, "Are you are Virgo?"

Elated that she almost picked his star sign, he replied, "Close. Libra. Although I do believe that being born September the 26th means I am very close to the cusp."

Then she screwed her face up, "No offence Paul." Her voice got higher, "Can I call you Paul?"

He bowed his head which she took as permission.

"It seems so unfair doesn't it that we are blessed with wisdom the moment our hips start aching and our nose spreads. I spend more time plucking my chin these days than anything else."

They both laughed. It was just a pity he did not see the genuine smile underneath the veil.

Chants from outside alerted them that it was almost time for his balcony performance.

"I hate Sundays," he growled.

They laughed again.

"I apologise that I cannot stay longer I would have liked to have gotten to know you better. I enjoy practicing my English. Latin however…can I be rude, a terribly complexed language. I am sure we are all bluffing when we say we understand it. But they tell me you are from Scotland. Forgive me but your accent is not clear."

"I have travelled somewhat. My mother was German. This has compromised my accent."

He looked at her puzzled and somewhat unsure.

"It was a pleasure to meet you Nicneven. It always delights me to meet an Ancient Witch, especially the very, very, very old ones," he winked.

"Enough with the old."

Nicneven turned and walked towards the door. She sensed he was a good-hearted man who actually cared for his people, and had a healthy relationship with God.

Before she reached the door, he called out to her. Turning on her heel, she faced him, "Yes?"

"In the future. In a thousand years from now."

"Yes?"

"Let it be known I truly wanted peace."

She nodded and left the room.

Following the security guard, she regretted wearing high heels as the sound of her steps echoed down the hall, making her feel quite exposed in a place that was foreign to her, after all she was there secretly.

Looking down an adjacent hall, Nicneven noticed at least eight security guards holding the latest firearms and wearing full body military armour. Whoever they were protecting in that wing was more important than the Pope.

"Who are they protecting?"

"That is confidential."

"Then why tell me it's confidential?"

She heard him grunt.

"Is that where the Black Pope is?"

This time he remained quiet.

"You know not replying means yes."

Still he remained quiet.

He heard her grunt.

For what seemed like two hours- but in reality was fifteen minutes, they walked through a myriad of halls and deadlocked doors until they reached HER door. Noticeably, not a security guard was seen anywhere.

Like a wave of euphoria, Nicneven removed her veil and shoes as instructed. In just moments, she would be in the arms of an old friend and in the presence of Isis, the only remaining Witch of the Original Coven.

Wanting to flirt with the security guard, she was disappointed as his eyes remained firmly at the door.

"Serious fellow aren't you?"

Moving in closely to him, her nipples poking through her dress, she touched his back with her breasts. She felt his body tense as he contemplated reaching for his rifle.

"Turn around Mr. Security Guard."

Knowing too well that he was unable to defend himself against the Witch, he did as she commanded.

Grabbing his right hand, she flipped his hand over and studied his palm. Surprisingly, his palms were soft and deep like a well and the lines clearly visible and thick.

"Palms hold secrets," she laughed. "Your palm tells me, you've never killed a man in your life and you go home to a nice boring wife and moisturise."

Looking up at him, she screwed her nose up, "To be honest, I find human palms totally revolting. No Magick in them at all."

"Do you think I'm here for your amusement?"

"Oh no. I don't think it," she cackled.

Raising her hand, she placed her palm in front of his face, "See my palm. It contains great stories. Stories to repeat, write down and remember. Stories told around the crackling of a fire. I've killed men like you. I don't tell you this to torment you, just want you to gain some perspective. See, you thought you were protecting me while the whole time it was I, protecting you."

Unnerved, he cocked his head to the side and chewed on the inside of his cheeks so to not provoke a scene with a sharp and focused, "Fuck you!"

And as if 'timing was divine' the door opened.

Forgetting the security guard, Nicneven walked towards Garnet-Ember and unlike most greetings, she instead rested her forehead against the Black Priestess' forehead in an Ancient Witch Greeting.

"Nicneven my love. What joy this brings me. The Goddesses will be rejoicing today."

Speaking as if whispering, a hushed parody as her voice echoed nothing but undiluted enthusiasm, Garnet-Ember was the poshest English Witch she knew.

Nicneven was overjoyed to see her.

The Black Priestess was an image of extravagance. Embracing her voluminous hourglass figure, her feminine oozed grandeur in her swing dance style frock, assessorised with large chunky silver jewellery and leopard-print throw that hung over one shoulder while teasing the other. Her eyes demanded attention. Large upturned grey-blue eyes framed steep, arched shaped, black eyebrows. Her hair was almost a 'manic panic' outrageous orange that accentuated the untidiness of the short scrunched hairstyle that Garnet-Ember would call the 'unruly aristocrat'. Painted bright red, her oversized lips expressed a wild sexuality that mesmerised all those who listened to her speak. Her cheeks glowed as if she had just fucked a man outside. Her skin dictated a healthy existence or the latest beauty technique. Italy was indeed perfect for a English Witch's complexion.

"You look like Betty Boop," Nicneven jested.

Stepping backwards, Garnet-Ember studied Nicneven's body.

"Nicneven your wrists and ankles are so thin, they look as if they might snap at any moment."

Then unexpectedly placing her palm on Nicneven's stomach, she listened, "You're Magick is still strong Nicneven. What is your most recent name now? No! Actually, please do not tell me. I hate all these modern names. Forgive me but I will continue to call you by the name I know you as. Come. I want you to meet her. Isis is in the garden."

Nicneven noticed her heartbeat skipped a little in anticipation of meeting a First Born. A true ascendant to the Goddess.

"I want you to meet someone close to my heart and the actual stonemason of this very auspicious room. He really is a talent. Have you ever seen such craftsmanship?"

The detail of the stone-craft was unfaultable. A true craftsmanship of passion and skill. The granite pillars stood five metres high and held up the cathedral ceilings that were decorated with the carved images of the Original Coven.

"As a young boy he walked a cow to market and bought a motorbike and rode straight to Rome where he scored- by chance in a coffee shop- the chance to train as a stonemason."

Overwhelmed by the images of the Original Coven, Nicneven focused on the carving of Mary. Palms clasped together as if praying, she was in fact recharging her own Magick to rejuvenate herself. After all, Witches were great healers. They had even taught Jesus to do it while telling him wonderful philosophies from Asia.

Garnet-Ember nodded, "Did it by hand. Fucking incredible."

"Truly magnificent."

"Isis speaks of the Original Coven often as if they stood in front of her, even after all these years. Isis strategically placed the Original Coven's essence into all the religions across the earth to keep their Magick alive. It pains her that the feminine energy is peripheral but she knows better than anyone the importance of keeping the truth hidden. Imagine living for over four thousand years? Never reincarnating? Why did the Darkness keep her alive? Poor humans, they have no idea of the truth. Isis even created the 'Witch' stereotype. She admits the Bible took a while to write but she is very proud of it. Guilt is a terrible burden. She never got over fucking up the greatest spell ever cast. Works diligently to make amends with her guilt. I remind her often that the spell worked somewhat. The world would be ruled by aliens now instead of Witches and we would all be red haired. The protection circle they created, even though thin, has created the most useful white light that we can tap into."

Grabbing Nicneven by her hand, Garnet-Ember walked her over to a set of two seater wicker couches that faced each other, with a matching wicker table with a glass top to separate them. A large fruit and cheese platter consumed most of the table and a bottle of French champagne was uncorked.

The peripheral view of the large indoor pool, enticed a sweaty Nicneven. Flying had dried her skin out and she was feeling parched.

Sitting down, Nicneven looked at the room again as it was not what she had imagined it to look like. Pastel green rendered walls soften the glare of the pool and unlike the rest of the Vatican there were no pieces of artwork to decorate the walls. The glass wall at the end of the pool framed a garden so still that for a moment, Nicneven thought it was an oil painting.

Garnet-Ember interrupted Nicneven's daydreaming, "She wanted to replicate the Hanging Garden of Babylon. Has one of the best irrigation systems in the world. Hmmm, just so she can feel part of nature. Cost a small fortune. I find gardening quite tedious. Over twelve landscapers tend to that garden a week. You wouldn't know due to how it looks."

It was hard to take in the detail of the garden at first. More chaotic than an overgrown secret garden, Nicneven was surprised any gardener tended to such a mess. The multitudes of exotic plants fought for natural light and Nicneven was reminded of the principle of natural selection as they all looked as if they were strangling each other. Vines of all colours, dropped down through large pergolas creating paths and dead spots. Many bees buzzed as they pollinated the flowers. Small trickles of water from the water features failed to add a sense of tranquility, and the razor sharp imported grasses that covered the ground would make it a treacherous activity to walk barefooted across. It was hard to believe that in the middle of the Vatican a garden could exist. Only a subtle fragrance drifted through the open doors to perfume the room.

Garnet-Ember spoke, "Isis has been very distant lately. Homesick. Missing ancient times. You understand? What are we without a Coven?"

Nicneven swung around to face Garnet-Ember, "An enslaved Non-Ancient," she teased.

Shocked by her unashamed attitude towards Non-Ancients, Garnet-Ember forced a smile upon her face.

The side door opened and a man walked in.

Garnet-Ember's face lit up, "Nicneven, this is Gianni, the stonemason."

As she stood up to shake hands, she noticed she stood at least a head and shoulders taller than the seventy 'something' year old Italian stonemason. Handsome with thick silver hair that he brushed back to form a wave, and a bronze complexion that complimented his round face and dark brown eyes, he came off as a jolly man.

"Bella Witch, it is a pleasure to meet you. You look fantastic for someone who has travelled so far and by Witches' broom, no?"

"I travel frequently to see my family. Flying by broom keeps the cobwebs at bay."

As if suddenly energised, Gianni sat down beside Garnet-Ember and brought attention to the platter of food on the table while pouring a champagne almost immediately. Passing it to Nicneven before she had a chance to decline his hospitality, he was overjoyed to be serving her, "Eat! Drink! Such pleasures must be indulged. Witches believe this, no?"

Garnet-Ember gave Nicneven a sympathetic look, "Humour him. He's a feeder. Likes a Witch with meat on her hips," she winked.

Not wanting to be rude, she took a sip, "Grazie."

The champagne bubbles tickled her nose and she reacted by giggling.

The sound of splashing alerted them that Isis had swam underneath the gap that linked the outside to the indoor pool.

Nicneven's heart skipped as she saw Isis grab the railing and pull herself out of the water.

A gasp choked Nicneven's throat as her eyes fell upon Isis. Spellbound in HER magnificence, Nicneven was enchanted.

As a Maiden she had fantasised about the Original Coven. A Coven as old as time. The first born Witches from the Goddess before she was split into four quarters. Those who created Atlantis and those who destroyed it. Their every cell whispering earthly truths, and the All-Seeing Eye that sees everything. An aura so bright that it glows white around her bronzed skin. A Magick so commanding that if you listen you can hear it humming a thousand moons away. An essence so pure that everything else in the room looks synthetic, and an energy so radiant that the only respectful action is to collapse upon your knees and pledge your absolute obedience.

The magnificence of the room only moments before, now paled in comparison as Isis stood in front of her. Beads of water sliding down her naked body made her look even more radiant. Seven feet tall, her wet thick black hair hung to the back of her thighs, which pulled her forehead tightly from the weight. The one large eye that sat in the middle of her forehead was made up only of a black iris and pupil, which flickered red as if flames existed within it, and the arrow head symbol (a triangle with the bottom side missing) encompassed the eye. Every muscle was well-defined, so much so that her skin looked at if it had been pulled so tightly over the muscle that it thinned and pinched like a seam, threatening to tear at any moment. Her breasts were heavy but sat up as if a child never feed from them, and her feet and hands were as large as any man's. Ochre coloured cheekbones sat high above her cheeks, and her lips were so black that they looked purple. But what Nicneven could not deny was the sadness hidden within her posture. Her spine may have been strong but the slight bend of her neck exposed a relentless and unforgiving nightmare that she was trapped within the Vatican. Trapped to rule the earth, alone.

Body shaking, and overwhelmed, Nicneven unexpectedly burst into tears. Never had she seen such sacredness.

"I apologise. To show such vulnerability is unforgiveable. I'm terribly overwhelmed."

Stepping across the marbled floor, every movement orchestrated and defined, Isis stood in front of Nicneven and spoke, and to Nicneven's fascination, a million Witch voices left Isis' lips. Nicneven closed her eyes. She could hear them all. Nicneven could even hear her own voice.

Nicneven suddenly realised that Isis held inside all the voices of Time, and indiscriminately, Isis loved them all. But there were twelve voices that she did not speak, for the voices of Kali, Mary, Sophia, Ishtar, Hathor, Tara, Lilith, Fatima, Orisha, Maman Brigitte, Abonde, and Circe were with the Darkness, suffering more than any Witch had ever suffered, condemned to live eternity within Gaia's stomach.

In absolute gratefulness, Nicneven found the strength to speak, "All Seeing-Eye, Isis, it is my absolute pleasure to meet you. This is a dream come true. Never in my wildest imagination did I think I would ever meet you. Ever."

"Isis is You and You are Isis. I am just a figure head to focus your attention," and then, stretching her arm out, she placed her hand on Nicneven's head. It was lucky Nicneven was sitting as her knees would have buckled from the sheer pleasure, and as if she was experiencing a thousand orgasms, an overpowering feeling of love and relaxation overcame Nicneven. Had she been able to, she would have closed her eyes and slept for days.

Isis smiled as if she was privy to Nicneven's past, and then lifted her hand off her head and walked off, exiting through the door Gianni had entered.

Like a school girl meeting her idol, Nicneven giggled, "Oh my Goddess, what was that?"

Grabbing three pieces of cheese and squashing them onto a cracker and then into his mouth, Gianni jested with a full mouth, "Without the ability to blink, I really don't know how she sleeps?"

Garnet-Ember rolled her eyes.

Looking at Gianni, Nicneven was unsure to laugh or not. She was still feeling euphoric from meeting Isis and hoped it would last for as long as it could. It was not that often that she felt this good.

Garnet-Ember interrupted, "We need to discuss what it is you're here for. As much as I wish this was a social engagement it unforgiveable is not I hear."

Nicneven nodded, but deep down the adrenaline was unbalancing her composure.

Surprisingly, Nicneven noticed Gianni was gently rubbing the outside of Garnet-Ember's knee cap with his index finger. Then, as if he had noticed Nicneven staring, he turned his attentions to her by intimately studying her black dress, beyond what Nicneven considered to be socially acceptable.

Nicneven asked, "Yes, Gianni?"

He instantly responded as if he had decided his reply moments earlier, "Why do Witches always wear black?"

Uncomfortable, Nicneven crossed her right leg over the other, while sliding further back on the couch to be as far away from Gianni's curiosity.

Reaching out, Garnet-Ember grabbed her glass of champagne and took an exaggerated sip. It was not the first time Gianni had taken a great interest in the female guests.

Squinting, Nicneven replied, "Some Witches are brave enough to wear the colour of their hearts on the outside."

And on cue, Gianni chuckled. His head moved side to side as if he was shaking off a persistent fly and it was then that Nicneven noticed that he had lost most of his teeth, exposing a humble upbringing or a sweet tooth.

Enjoying the conversation, Gianni responded cheekily, "I hear you are married Nicneven. I tried that once."

"Ah, but did you try hard enough?" She jested.

This time, Garnet-Ember laughed, "He has tried many times Nicneven. Slow learner."

Not afraid of responsive banter, he replied, "Wives are the most dangerous creatures on the planet? I escaped three wives with only the hat on my head."

"Left his pants at the other woman's house," Garnet-Ember added.

Instead of laughing Nicneven uncrossed her legs and then as if on slow-play, crossed the other leg over her other knee and stared at Gianni. Although she wanted to remain juvenile, Gianni's attitude surprisingly triggered anger in her.

"I think Gianni, that the most dangerous creature in the world is a Witch!"

Bending from the waist to add drama, she focused on the randy little Italian man, "The greatest threat to a man is a Witch who is loyal to her authentic self, and who has a Coven to help her achieve it. Beware Gianni, for a Witch who has found her Coven is unstoppable. She is something to fear and worship on your quivering knees while you piss your pants. Men bend at a Witch's will or die, and always remember this, Witches may have been born in the dirt, but they will consume a man's whole fucking world, every time."

Delighted with such fierceness, Gianni shoved another piece of cheese in his mouth and giggled, "Bellissimo."

Nicneven fought the urge to jump on the table, placing one knee on top of his beloved cheese and stabbing him in the eye with a fork. Why do men always belittle a female's mind? *Fuck him!* She had showed him strength and he thought she was cute. He might as well have patted her on the head like a puppy dog. The righteous prick thought so little of her that even when she spoke the truth, a truth that she earned to speak, he was still loyal to his misguided belief of who he thought females were. In that moment, she fucking hated him, and any happiness she had felt after meeting Isis disappeared.

"My speech wasn't for your entertainment, Gianni. You would be wise to start using your big ears to hear properly when a Witch speaks. Maybe what a man really wants is a meek woman who is gullible and fragile? Good luck finding one of them after the age of twenty seven. Because I find when a man has a strong woman, or Witch, they do their best to destroy the empowerment in which they were so attracted to in the first place, as if scared of it, as if the woman or Witch had pretended to be someone else. Then…the man torments her mind until he has her believing she is crazy. I love being a Maiden. A time of naivety. A time to believe the bullshit. Awakened is cruel. Our cells are built on resentment."

Surprised by Nicneven's verbal attack, he choked a little of his cracker, "Oh how it must feel to tame a Witch."

Upset, Garnet-Ember raised her hand, as if the small hand gesture could erase the tension between Gianni and Nicneven. It was however forceful enough for Nicneven to realise she had gone too far, after all she was a guest and she had only just met Gianni.

Garnet-Ember studied Nicneven. Known to speak with integrity and venom in former speeches, Garnet-Ember was not surprised by the passionate display of assertiveness she had just witnessed but she heard an unfamiliar quiver upon the tone. A display of sorrow, rattling and coated with phlegm. Rarely a trait of an Ancient Witch. Garnet-Ember suddenly felt troubled. It would appear the flexibility required of constantly being reincarnated was also affecting Nicneven.

"You are both wrong," Garnet-Ember intervened, "The most dangerous person on the earth is, she or he, who does not value those things outside of themselves. The traveller is not a concern for us as she values experience and spends most of her time searching for it. The wonderer is romantic but will eventually settle on a home once she feels a sense of love and commitment to a place. The gypsy is terrifying but also harmless as she values those things which do not belong to her and therefore spend most of her time busy with stealing. It is those who do not value what the world has to offer them who are the most dangerous. For those people cannot be persuaded or manipulated, not tempted with gold or money, or bound up with religious guilt or family responsibility. They consider themselves completely whole and free from all restraints. They see the ropes I have tied around them and they step straight out of them. They value their own eyes and instincts. They see themselves equal to Gaia. They walk a path of self, as if one with the whole bloody universe. It is those people, lucky enough for us, who we can call crazy and mad, and treat them harshly or send them to mental asylums. Confusing their thoughts is the best prison of all, why do you think men do that to women? Times may change. Cultures may evolve but the root of evil remains. We know women are logical and not controlled by emotion. So now men use science and say they are mentally ill instead. Women aren't mentally ill, they're angry...

Getting back to the uncontrollable- those who are followed and praised by the masses, like musicians, we find someone to assassinate them. Sends the most wonderful shock wave of trauma through society. If stupid humans ever discover the intricate truth that their reality is coordinated by me and the All-Seeing Eye, how free they would feel. Finally, they would know how entrapped they are and surely rejoice? Don't get me wrong, humans are great at causing their own misery but we control education, banks, governments, wars, everything. So I suppose, we control the whole fucking world."

"It's hard to believe," Nicneven asked inquisitively.

Garnet-Ember sighed, "That it's all been a game? A time-waster? That their precious lives mean nothing? That there is no reason for their existence except that we need them to populate like the cattle they are and die, and it's not their bodies we want but their souls. Sooner they fill up heaven the sooner God will be released."

Chewing on her tongue, Nicneven attempted to relax. Forcibly dropping her shoulders and slouching to hide her enthusiasm, she was sure it was obvious that she was indeed experiencing a heightened keenness for the conversation, after all, she wanted to know the truth more than anyone and the truth was being freely spoken of in-between these walls.

"We need to fill Gaia's mind up. A huge population of humans are required for that. So we funnel money into better health care and hygiene in the Western countries that is actually making them more sick, while the poor bastards in the third world countries or what I call 'the breeders' are birthing and dying in huge quantities. It's like a fucking gold mine in Africa. But humans have brains that need entertaining, so we give them things to do, to strive for. Our own little matrix, but once heaven is filled up and our uncle is released from the pearly gates of his prison, we have quite a welcoming party arranged for him."

Gianni responded quite deviously, "That would make a great movie title, 'The Matrix.'"

"That would be a terrible movie title," Garnet-Ember retaliated.

Suddenly, everything that seemed important to Nicneven was irrelevant. She had flown from England with such conviction of purpose and now after hearing these revelations, she felt quite naive. What a beautifully thought-out plan. Humans were the flies to catch the spider.

Gianni spoke as if he was privy to all matters, "It is true. For over four thousand years every historical event has been orchestrated by Isis. You see she wants her Coven back, and she wants her uncle as a bargaining tool. If God likes it or not, once heaven reaches its' quota, out he comes. And to be honest, he's literally fucked the moment his feet touch the ground."

Garnet-Ember continued the revelations, "We are very close to the quota. And luckily, it will be within our lifetime. The moment the humans meet God, we bring him down to his knees and finally reveal ourselves as the all- Magickal owners of Gaia."

Nicneven grabbed her champagne flute and gulped down the remainder of her drink. Usually clear of thought, she was experiencing a 'foggy' brain.

"Let me get this clear. What if the humans turn on the Witches? Every soul ever created will be released as well. Sounds dangerous to me. We are outnumbered."

Blinking several times before answering, Garnet-Ember realise she had revealed too much and wanted to recoil from the conversation, "Leave the details to us. Isis has had four thousand years to plan God's return."

Gianni interrupted, "Heaven must be full of arseholes. Humans don't change their personality when they die. There is no sudden realisation or enlightenment. A bastard alive, a bastard dead. Must be a shit-fight up there. When they reach heaven I bet they wish they hadn't been such ignorant stupid people their entire lives and spent their time on evolving."

"You mean in Gaia's mind?" Nicneven snarled at Gianni.

Garnet-Ember quickly defended Gianni, "Heaven is so much easier to say then Gaia's mind. Side note, do you see your Coven much?"

Nicneven replied uneasily, "You know, we get so busy with life we forget the importance of physical contact. All of us run successful businesses. Miss large chunks of years chasing dreams and raising our children. We skip large ceremonies and rituals. It pains me to say, that I haven't seen my Coven in many years."

Garnet-Ember softened, "I hear this from everyone. I must make note to rectify this situation. It is most important that we continue to build the feminine connection, for our energies, and general happiness are pivotal for our future. We need to be a strong force when the time is right. I mean, have we become so self-efficient that we can manifest and spell without support? No! If we don't have our female friends, what do we have?"

Nicneven shivered, "Men."

Gianni nodded as if he understood the depth of the sarcasm.

However it was time to discuss the reason Nicneven had travelled over a thousand miles for.

"There is plot to overthrow the Highest Priestess and the Sisters of the Moon, and the Head Covens in every country, by a Non-Ancient Witch named Aggie. I'm here to ask your permission for you to turn a blind eye to this…literally? Let's say I am invested in her rise to power."

"That's adorable."

"Excuse me?"

"You're here to ask permission. Oh Nicneven, the All-Seeing Eye sees everything. We've been watching Aggie for a very long time now. Needless to say, we are very busy, we do miss fucking stuff."

Raising her hand to her mouth, Garnet-Ember laughed, "Excuse my language, I've been spending too much time with the Cardinals lately. They swear like sailors."

Eager to learn of the Black Pope, Nicneven asked, "Who is the Black Pope these days?"

Shuffling on the couch, Garnet-Ember chuckled, "That is confidential as his role is to oversee the Elite, and the Elite can get sensitive about details being shared. I can tell you this though, he's a prick. It will be hard to replace him when he retires. He has a certain…skill of mastermind and he is a hard worker. Speaks directly with the Elite which is a talent. I find the Elite infuriatingly boring. They are consumed with purity and bloodlines. If there was such a creature as a vampire it is the Elite. The Black Pope was a Financial Advisor before we promoted him. Couldn't care less about Goddesses or the cause, but if the figures don't add up, watch out. It is all about profit. The Elite think the Black Pope is the figurehead. God forbid, pun intended, when the Elite find out Isis is the big boss. Although, Isis is more concerned with swimming these days."

Gianni interrupted, "At times, we do steal the conspiracy theorist's ideas. Such madness they create. I say to Garnet-Ember, 'those conspiracy theorist we should hire them to work for us,' and she say, 'Gianni they already do,' and we laugh."

Unamused Garnet-Ember replied, "Gianni is like my 'comedic wingman,' although not funny at all."

Nicneven's took the opportunity to ask, "What do you think of the Non-Ancients? What is their purpose?"

"Winking at Gianni, Garnet-Ember replied, "Like everyone's purpose."

"Which is?"

"To help us gain world domination. To create one world. Our world. Even the most insignificant creature has its place in the wholeness of being and the righteous cause."

"What is the cause?"

"To eliminate the humans, God, and the Darkness, and allow us without interference to be the rightful caretakers of Gaia, and bring her back into balance. To be honest, it brings me such joy to see the apes miserable. And I will miss them, stupid little fucks. I mean, they still believe in the Devil while the Darkness eats their children. Dumb cunts. Sorry, swearing again. Good news though, which will free up some of my time, we are creating at the moment a time-waster called the Wide World Network, or something like that, to be released in ten years. It's fascinating. Magick at your fingertips. We will be able to snoop and collect information in every home in the world. Bless the author George Orwell and his book 'Nineteen Eighty-Four' for giving us the idea. It will be a great distraction."

"Matrix," Gianni laughed.

"Enough with the Matrix, Gianni. It's a fucking stupid name for a movie," Garnet-Ember scolded.

"Wouldn't it be easier to let the Darkness finish the humans off?"

"And feed the Darkness up to challenge us. Oh no. We are happy for them to loiter in the corners of children's bedrooms because the hole in Gaia's stomach is getting bigger. The Darkness has caused an ulcer in her stomach from all its bitterness. Gaia needs a good anti-inflammatory or probiotic."

"Why did the Original Coven protect the humans from the Red Haired Men four thousand years ago?"

"The Original Coven were protecting Gaia, not the humans."

"Nicneven, I've known you a long time but I have never been able to tell you these truths. I'm glad I can share them with you now. I want to protect you somehow from the potential terror but I also need to ask you to protect someone. The Soul-mates are estimated to be born again soon. Let's say we have helped with the process. Chosen the right Witch to be her mother, but we need you to keep an eye on the Soul-mate Witch as she grows up. We need her head to remain on her shoulders."

Sitting back, dropping her shoulders as if she was practicing relaxation, Garnet-Ember spoke again, "There are signs Gaia is waking."

A cold shiver ran down Nicneven's spine.

Nicneven took a deep breath and then pursed her lips to exhale.

Garnet-Ember raised both her eyebrows, "The snow is melting. Our great creator, our Grandmother is stirring up quite a scene in Antarctica. We've had the Germans down there since the First World War to keep an eye on it, while also looking for any potential 'landings' by the Red Haired Men. Don't get me wrong, the earth has its cycles. They think it's global warming, but it's the humans creating it with their thoughts. Not car fumes or factories but their own negativity. I suppose we have to take responsibility for that. It's a delicate situation, we need to fill up heaven as soon as possible before Gaia awakes. The world is out of balance. Just because we are Witches doesn't mean we don't understand science. Fuck, we brought science to the world! It's all about vibration baby. It's Witches that understand how energy works better than any scientist, but the signs are quite distinct this time. It all makes sense. Heaven is nearly full. The Darkness is feeding well on human negativity, while the same negativity is making Gaia sick in her stomach. We are what we eat after all. And down to the last minute, we have planned the surprise attack to end the family rivalry. But we need the triad whole again. Three sides of the triangle back together. Conditions must be perfect. The Darkness left us with a mathematical symbol, ^," she laughed, "We are ready to make the triangle whole again, then abolish it forever. There is so much concern for duality but empowerment comes from the power of three and the universal number nine. Isis wants her Coven back. Isis believes that it the Original Coven, particularly Sophia, is trying to escape the Darkness, and this is upsetting the equilibrium vibration which is causing Gaia to wake from her slumber. Last time she woke it was total devastation. Nothing survived."

Gianni unexpectedly reverted the conversation back to the reason Nicneven was there, "Aggie, quit an exquisite Non-Ancient. I am feeling positively enamoured with her ambitions."

"You've always been partial to a red-head, Gianni," snapped Garnet-Ember.

They all laughed.

Garnet-Ember shuffled to the edge of the couch, "You have our permission. We support Aggie in her adventures. It will keep the Ancients busy for a few years, and to be honest maybe teach the Ancients to stop being such arseholes."

Offended, Nicneven managed to nod graciously.

Garnet-Ember continued, "One of the most outstanding accomplishments of living for eternity, is how diminutive your tolerance is for liars. In the beginning, you hope the person in front of you is respectful enough to speak only the truth. After a sobering amount of consistent betrayal, you tend to wait a little before making a judgement of a person's character. A few more acts of blatant lying and you find yourself positively resentful, and start to believe everyone is dishonest, but truthfully, no one can live like that. Best to toughen, not harden. You start to notice the pitch in someone's voice, the high octave on the edge of the deceit, the whisper as they attempt to hide the larger lies. You notice the eye twitch and the exaggeration of detail. It helps to know them well of course. The smallest deviation of habit or behavior and your body feels the impact like a sudden heat wave. We all lie. It's part of survival. Some embellish the story, others boost their low self-esteem with acts of made-up accolades, others hid the truth of their pasts so they can move forwards without judgement, and others tell little lies to save another person's feelings. It's those who lie to themselves that are the most dangerous. Their voice does not quiver and they can look at you, deep, deep inside your eyes and without guilt, shatter your life."

Nicneven tensed. What was Garnet-Ember implying?

"But really Nicneven….you're a fantastic liar. Always have been. It's one of the things I adore about you. But are you sure Aggie hasn't sensed your betrayal?"

Sitting up, back straight, shoulders at ear height, Nicneven laughed, "You know already?"

"The All-Seeing Eye knows all. It's like Gossip central here at the Vatican. Males are the best gossipers of all though. You've brought us a present," Gianni declared.

Garnet-Ember's glanced at Nicneven's bag, "Come on then. Show us."

Letting out a relieved laugh, Nicneven opened the bag to reveal a very large book.

Gianni sat up so abruptly that he almost fell off the couch to get a better look.

"Well, well, well. It's been a long time since I've seen the Ancient Doctrine. It looks as if it hasn't been read in three thousand years."

Nicneven sighed, "I wish I could say it hadn't. Aggie doesn't know of Isis' existence. I can't have this falling into the hands of a Non-Ancient. Sorry but I just can't. Aggie is determined to rule the World. She would come after Isis next and the information in this would seal our fate. I've never seen determination in a Witch. Aggie is a phenomenon, but I can't tolerate her obtaining such knowledge, especially since it really belongs to Isis. I'm returning it to its rightful owner. After all, it was the only item saved from Atlantis, and hopefully, it will help Isis rescue her Coven from the Darkness. At times, I may lack values and morals, but I am an Ancient, loyal to the Original Coven, loyal to the Beginning."

Gianni enjoying the conversation, sprung off the couch, "I must know your modern name? I must!"

Jaide winked, "Somethings are better kept secret."

I hope you enjoyed the first novella of three.

Thank you for your patience as I write WAND^.

Jo Green.

2017.

Main books of the Series

S^ORD
Book One

***

WAND^
Book Two

***

^CUP
Book Three

***

PEN^TACLE
Book Four